Slop!

A Welsh Folktale

Retold by
Margaret Read MacDonald

Illustrated by
Yvonne LeBrun Davis

fulcrum kids
Golden, Colorado

An old man and an old woman once lived in
a little house with a fence all around their yard.

Every evening when old woman cooked
dinner, she peeled the potatoes ... and tossed the
peelings in the slop bucket.

Slop!

She peeled the carrots ... and tossed the
peelings in the slop bucket.

Slop!

She peeled the onions ... and tossed the
peelings in the slop bucket.

Slop!

She and the old man sat down to good
vegetable stew.
    Then she washed the dishes ... and
poured the dishwater in the slop bucket.
    Slop!
    "Husband!
Carry out the slops!"

The old man picked up the heavy bucket of slops
and carried it out the front door.
He staggered just ten steps.
1—2—3—4—5—*6-7-8-9-10!*

Slop!

He threw it over the front fence.
Old man did this every night, but one night ...

"I wish you would stop doing that!"
The old man looked all around but didn't see a thing.
"I said, I WISH you would stop doing that!"
And there at his feet was a wee little man!
"MUST you pour slops down my chimney every evening?"
"But I pour my slops over the garden wall."
"And onto MY house!" said the little man.

The old man peered over the garden wall.
He didn't see anything but rocks and weeds and slops.
"Would you like to see with my eyes?" asked the little man.
"Then put your foot on MY foot and look again."
So the old man very gently put his big foot on top of the wee man's little foot and peered over the garden wall once more.

There was a wee little cottage!
And, oh my goodness, peelings hung from the roof.
Peelings covered the yard.
And dirty dishwater ran down the chimney and out the door!
"I've been pouring my slops down your chimney!" said the old man.
"And I wish you would stop doing that!" said the little man.

The old man went back into his house and told his wife what he had seen.

"And the little man's wife has to mop up dirty dishwater and sweep out the peelings every day!"

"That poor woman!" said his wife. "We must stop pouring our slops down their chimney."

"But where shall we pour them?" said the old man. "The bucket is so heavy. I could never manage to carry it around to the back garden wall to dump it."

They sat and thought.

Then the old woman had an idea.

"If we had a door at the BACK of the house, you could walk just ten steps out the BACK door. We can hire the carpenter to make us a new back door."

"That will cost money. We have very little of that."

"I have a bit put by," said the old woman. "And I will be glad to spend it to make our neighbors happy."

So the door was made.

And that evening the old woman peeled her potatoes and tossed the peelings in the slop bucket.

Slop!

She peeled her carrots and tossed the peelings in the slop bucket.

Slop!

She peeled her onions and tossed the peelings in the slop bucket.

Slop!

After they ate their good vegetable stew, she washed the dishes and poured the dishwater in the slop bucket.

Slop!

"Husband!
Carry out the slops!"

The old man picked up the slop bucket.
He turned and went out the BACK door.
1—2—3—4—5—*6-7-8-9-10!*

Slop!

Right over the BACK fence.
Then he listened.

"Thank you, neighbor!"
A good place for a compost heap.

The old woman and the old man had spent their savings on a new back door, but they never lacked for anything after all.

For every evening, when the old man opened the back door ... a small gold coin would roll in.

Clink ... clink ... clink ... clink ... clink.

It was left there by the little man.

A gift from one good neighbor to another.

About the Folktale

This Welsh folktale is retold from "Slops" in *Peace Tales: World Folktales to Talk About* by Margaret Read MacDonald (Hamden, Conn.: Linnet Books, 1992). Other versions can be found in *Welsh Legendary Tales* by Elisabeth Sheppard-Jones (Edinburgh: Thomas Nelson, 1959) and in *Fairy Tales from the British Isles* by Amabel Williams-Ellis (New York: Frederick Warne, 1960). This story contains folk motifs F235.5.1, *Fairies made visible by standing on another's foot,* and F340, *Gifts from fairies.*

About the Illustrations

The illustrations are done in multimedia on Arches HotPress paper. Because the story takes place in Wales, you might look for Welsh ponies, leeks (a national emblem), a Welsh vole, and a Welsh corgi throughout the illustrations.

About the Back Cover Illustration

There are many sources "confirming" the belief that the Welsh corgi's white fur across its shoulders is really a saddle to be used by wee folk. One source is the *New Complete Pembroke Welsh Corgi* by Deborah S. Harper (New York: Howell Bookhouse, 1979, 1994 revised), p. 1.

Text copyright © 1997 Margaret Read MacDonald
Illustrations copyright © 1997 Yvonne LeBrun Davis

Library of Congress Cataloging-in-Publication Data
MacDonald, Margaret Read
    Slop! : a Welsh folktale / retold by Margaret Read MacDonald ; illustrated by Yvonne LeBrun Davis.
      p.   cm.
    Summary: An old man and old woman throw their dinner leftovers unknowingly onto the tiny house of a little man and his wife.
    ISBN 1-55591-352-0 (hardcover)
    [1. Folklore—Wales.] I. Davis, Yvonne, ill. II. Title.
PZ8.1.M15924S1   1997
398.2'09429'02—dc21   96-53359
                                               CIP
                                              AC

Printed in Korea
0 9 8 7 6 5 4 3 2 1

Fulcrum Publishing
350 Indiana Street, Suite 350
Golden, Colorado 80401-5093
(800) 992-2908 • (303) 277-1623